The Bump in the Night

by ANNE ROCKWELL

SCHOLASTIC BOOK SERVICES
NEW YORK · TORONTO · LONDON · AUCKLAND · SYDNEY · TOKYO

ISBN 0-590-30071-7

12 11 10 9 8 7 6 5 4 3 2 1   10   9/7 0 1 2 3 4/8
Printed in the U.S.A.   07

CHAPTER 1

The Castle

Long ago

there was a castle.

It was old.

It was cold.

It was gray.

And it was haunted.

There was a ghost
in the castle.
There was a ghost
who went
BUMP in the night.
The ghost howled too.

No one went in the castle.

No one walked in
its garden.

No one picked
olives and oranges
from the trees
in its garden.

It was a haunted castle.

CHAPTER 2

Toby the Tinker

Toby the tinker
came to the castle.

Toby was a smart boy.
He could tinker this
and tinker that.
He could fix anything
that was broken.

He traveled from here

to there,

fixing this and

fixing that.

Tinkering and fixing,

that was what Toby did.

But mostly he tinkered

pots and pans.

And Toby was not afraid

of anything.

When Toby the tinker

saw the castle,

he said to himself,

"What a fine old castle.

I will stop here tonight.

Maybe the castle

is cold.

I will pick up

some sticks

and make a fire.

I have bacon and eggs

and pots and pans.

I will cook myself
some bacon and eggs
for supper."

Toby the tinker went into
the haunted castle.

CHAPTER 3

A Bump and a Howl

Toby the tinker

built a fire.

He put a pan

on the fire.

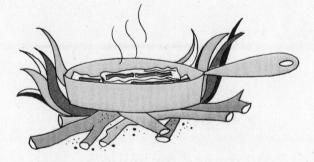

He put some bacon
in the pan.
The bacon sizzled
and cooked.
"Yum!" said Toby.
"How hungry I am!"

Just then Toby the tinker
heard something go
BUMP.

He heard something howl.

"Owwwwwwwwooooooo —

Look out!

I'm falling!"

Toby the tinker said,

"Well, fall where you will,

but don't put out my fire."

And the bacon sizzled

and cooked.

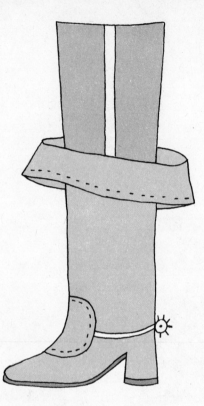

BUMP.
Down fell a leg
out of the chimney.
It landed right by
Toby the tinker.

"Well," said Toby,
who was not afraid
of anything,
"where is the rest
of you?"
But the leg
did not answer.
BUMP!
Something howled,
"Owwwwwwweeeeeee —
Look out!
I'm falling!"

"Fall where you will,"
said Toby the tinker,
"but don't break my eggs."

And the bacon sizzled
and cooked,
and down fell
another leg.

Then there was
another bump in the night.
Something howled,
"Owwwwwwwwwwwowowowow –
Look out!
I'm falling!"
Down fell a body
with two arms.
Toby the tinker broke
four eggs into the pan.

He said,

"I will fix you,"

to the legs

and the body.

So, as the bacon sizzled
and the eggs cooked,
Toby tinkered this
and tinkered that —

23

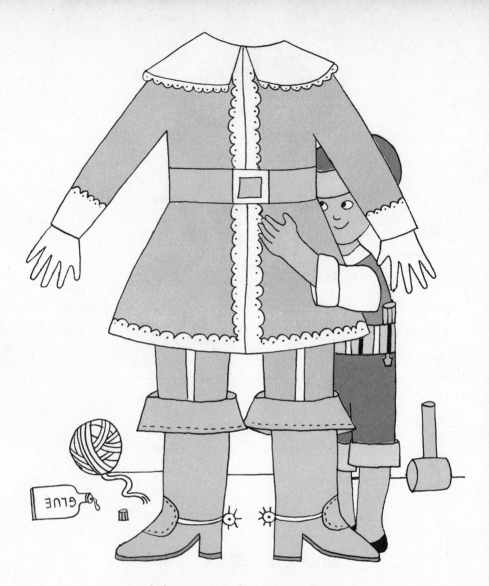

and he put the two legs

on the body.

"Now," he said,

"it is too bad

you have no head.

For if you did,

I would give you

some bacon and eggs."

And Toby the tinker

sat down to eat.

He was not afraid

of anything.

CHAPTER 4

The Ghost

Something went BUMP.

Something howled,

"Owwwwwwww –

Look out!

I'm falling!"

And down fell a head.

"Hello, head,"

said Toby the tinker.

He tinkered this
and tinkered that
and put the head
on the body.

"Now," he said,

"you are all fixed.

Have some bacon and eggs."

"Aren't you afraid of me?"

asked the ghost.

"I'm not afraid of anything,"
said Toby the tinker.
"But I am very hungry."
He ate his bacon and eggs.
The ghost ate some too.

Then the ghost said,
"Now that you have
fixed me and fed me,
I can go away.
But first
I want to reward you.
Come into the garden
with me."
So Toby did.

CHAPTER 5

Under the Olive Tree

"Once I was a rich man,"

said the ghost.

"Robbers robbed me.

I had one bag
of copper pennies.
I had one bag
of silver spoons.
And I had one bag
of twenty gold rings.
The robbers
chopped me up
and hid me in the castle.

They took

my copper pennies,

my silver spoons

and my twenty gold rings.

They buried them

under the olive tree.

But I howled and howled
and bumped and bumped
and the robbers
ran away.

I haunted the castle

and the robbers

were afraid to come back.

But, poor me,"

said the ghost,

and began to cry.

"Everyone was afraid of me.

When I howled

and went BUMP in the night,

people ran away.

How happy I am

that you did not run away.

What a smart boy you are!

How happy I am

that you tinkered this

and tinkered that

and put me together again."

The ghost pointed

to the olive tree

in the castle garden.

"Dig under that tree,"

it said

to Toby the tinker.

"Dig, and you will find

my bag of copper pennies,

my bag of silver spoons,

and my twenty gold rings.

The silver spoons

and the gold rings

are all for you,

because you fixed me.

I will keep

the copper pennies

and I will go away."

So Toby the tinker
and the fixed ghost
dug up the buried bags
of copper pennies,
silver spoons
and gold rings.

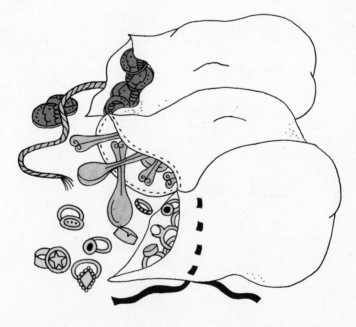

The ghost took
the copper pennies
and went away.

Toby the tinker
moved into the castle.

He tinkered this
and tinkered that.
He fixed everything
in the castle
that needed fixing.

He was rich
and he never, never
was afraid of anything.
The castle
was not haunted
anymore.
Everyone brought
pots and pans
to the castle
for fixing.

And Toby the tinker

was happy.

Very happy indeed.